My Dad's In Prison

by Jackie Walter and Tony Neal

W

FRANKLIN WATTS

LONDON·SYDNEY

Franklin Watts
First published in Great Britain in 2018 by
The Watts Publishing Group
Copyright © The Watts Publishing
Group 2018

Editor: Julia Bird
Illustrator: Tony Neal

HB ISBN 978 1 4451 6133 4
PB ISBN 978 1 4451 6132 7

Franklin Watts
An imprint of
Hachette Children's Group
Part of The Watts Publishing Group
Carmelite House
50 Victoria Embankment
London EC4Y 0DZ

An Hachette UK Company
www.hachette.co.uk
www.franklinwatts.co.uk

Printed in China

Dad wasn't at home when I got back from school. I was disappointed because I wanted to show him the dinosaur I painted in my art lesson.

Mum said I should have an early night because
it was swimming after school tomorrow.

Dad wasn't home after swimming, or the day after that.
Mum looked really sad. She said he had to stay away for a bit,
but he missed me. I miss him too.

Next day, Logan and I were having an argument.
He said I took his apple, but I didn't.
Then he said I was no better than my dad.

I felt really upset so I told my teacher.
"Where's my dad?" I asked him. Mr Jones said he wasn't
sure but that I should ignore Logan who was not being kind.
He talked to Logan as well, and to my mum
when it was home time.

Mum took me for a walk after school. She told me that Dad had broken the law, which is like breaking the rules. She said we all make mistakes sometimes. Now he has to spend some time in prison to show he is sorry.

I asked Mum when Dad was coming home, but she said she didn't know exactly. I'm really cross with him, but I miss him too.

Later, I asked Mum what it was like in a prison. She told me Dad has food at a canteen like we have in school, he can read books, and he has a room that he shares with another man called John.

He has exercise time when he can go outside and he can
watch TV too. He just can't come out to see us when he likes.
I asked if we could go and see him and she said yes, soon.
She said he still loved us and he always would.

I was worried that Dad might have taken some new trainers for me because I kept asking for them. But Mum said it wasn't that, and it wasn't my fault at all.

That night, I talked to Dad on the phone. He said he was sorry about not being there. I told him about Logan being mean.

Dad said I was to ignore people who said horrible stuff
as much as I could, and that he loved me.

I didn't want to go to school the next morning. Mum said Mr Jones would help me if I felt wobbly. I said I would hit anyone who said anything mean, but Mum said I was not to do that. "You just tell a teacher," she said, "but it might be all right. You are still the same boy you were before with the same friends. Next week, they'll all be talking about something else."

It was nice to be at school in the end. Nobody else said anything and I'm not sure who knows about Dad. Logan even said sorry to me. We just did the usual things we always do. It was good not to think about Dad for a while, but then I felt bad.

When I got home, I told Mum I felt bad for forgetting Dad at school. She laughed. "Do you normally think about Dad all the time when you are at school? I don't think so!"
Then she gave me a letter from Dad. I got one and so did she. He's written me a story. It made me happy, but it made me cry too.

Mum gave me an extra big hug and stroked my hair until I fell asleep.

A few weeks later, we go to visit Dad! My uncle picks us up early and we have to drive down a lane with big fences. There are lots of cameras and I feel nervous, but Mum says that we can have a chocolate bar when we get there. We are going to visit Dad in a sort of café. My uncle says he'll wait for us and to save him some chocolate.

Mum has to fill in loads of forms, then we have to walk through an arch and hold up our arms like aeroplanes while the officers wave a wand around us. Lastly, we go past some dogs and into a waiting room.

There's a boy there from football called Luke! He says he's going to see his dad, but he's hoping that this will be the last visit before his dad comes home. I never knew his dad was in prison, but Luke says he can't really remember his dad ever being at home before. I hope my dad isn't going to be away for that long.

After a while, we go into a big visitor room and sit at a table.
I can't see Dad, but Mum tells me not to worry. "He'll be here
soon," she says. "I'll bet he's excited to see you!"
Then I see Dad!

He walks over as fast as he can and scoops
me up, then gives Mum a kiss.

Mum goes to buy some drinks and chocolate. I don't know what to say at first, but Dad starts telling me all about the dinners he has (even cabbage which he hates as much as I do) and his room. Soon it's just like speaking to Dad again.

I promise to write back and ask him to keep sending the stories. I tell him I'll miss him, and he says he'll miss me more. Soon, the officers tell us that the visiting time is over and we have to say goodbye.

It's very quiet on the way home. It was so nice to see Dad. We're going to see him again in a few weeks, and I'll speak to him on the phone this week too. He's promised to send me another story in a letter, and I can't wait. My dad might be away from me right now, but he's still my dad and he always will be.

Advice for parents and carers

Having a parent or sibling go to prison can be traumatic for a child. How much you tell them will depend on the age of your child, as will how much they understand about what is going on.

Explaining the absence of their parent or sibling is a difficult conversation, so it might be helpful to find a quiet time. Try to go slowly, and in an age-appropriate way for your child. This will give it time to sink in and let them think of questions. These questions might involve why, where, when are they coming back and can we talk to them? You might want to think about how you would answer these questions before you have the conversation - even though you might not know all the answers.

The child's questions may not come at once - they may think of questions after the initial shock. Your child might feel very upset, angry, frustrated and even guilty. If your child is asked to keep it a secret, or if they decide to keep it a secret, this might also make them feel isolated and lonely. Your child will need loads of reassurance that you are not going anywhere, that you are happy to talk about everything and that they are free to tell you how they feel.

Keeping to your normal routines at this time can feel difficult, but it might help get some sense of normality back. Helping your child cope with any feelings of anger or anxiety might be of benefit. For example, you could encourage them to shout at or tell all their worries to a soft toy, write down or draw their worries, or make a plan together of what to do if they are anxious about a situation, such as being teased at school.

Try to let family or friends help, or look at organisations, such as Action for Prisoners' and Offenders' Families: (www.prisonersfamilies.org.uk). Your child's school can also help support your child. Childline counsellors can be useful for children if they wish to speak to someone outside of their usual circle.

Finally, it will be up to you how much contact you decide is appropriate between your child and their parent or sibling in prison. Depending on the situation, it can give great reassurance to both to maintain this relationship through letters, phone conversations and even potentially visits. Some prisons allow email to keep contact going.

About Storybook Dads:

Storybook Dads is a charity that works with parents in prison, enabling them to read and record bedtime story CDs, DVDs and other educational gifts to send to their children.

Find out more about the work of Storybook Dads: http://www.storybookdads.org.uk/ (Storybook Dads also operates in women's prisons).